W9-AAJ-318

Ei   234751
H   6.75

FOR SALE

Holland
A big ball of string

HQ   DATE DUE

mo

ST. CLOUD PUBLIC LIBRARY

GREAT RIVER REGIONAL LIBRARY

St. Cloud, Minnesota   56301

A Big Ball of String

Written and illustrated by

MARION HOLLAND

Beginner Books

A DIVISION OF RANDOM HOUSE, INC.

50 9695

To

NICK and ANDREW

This title was originally catalogued by the Library of Congress as follows: Holland, Marion. A big ball of string, written and illustrated by Marion Holland. [New York] Beginner Books; distributed by Random House [1958] 64 p. illus. 24 cm. I. Title. PZ8.3.H699Bi 58-11964 ISBN 0-394-80005-2 ISBN 0-394-90005-7 (lib. bdg.)

© Copyright, 1958, by Marion Holland. All rights reserved under International and Pan-American Copyright Conventions. Published in New York by Random House, Inc., and simultaneously in Toronto, Canada, by Random House of Canada, Limited. Manufactured in the United States of America.

I had a little string.

It was no good at all.

I went to look for more string

To make a string ball.

ST. CLOUD PUBLIC LIBRARY
234751

I got more string

From a box in the hall.

I made it all up

In a little string ball.

But what could I DO

With a little ball of string?

What could I do

With a SMALL string ball?

With a BIG ball of string,

I could do ANYTHING.

Anything, anything,

ANYTHING AT ALL!

My mother has string.

Look what a lot!

Did she give ME some of it?

She did NOT.

"Stay OUT
Of my things!"
Mother said,
With a frown.
"You can NOT
Have those strings.
Put them down!
Put them down!"

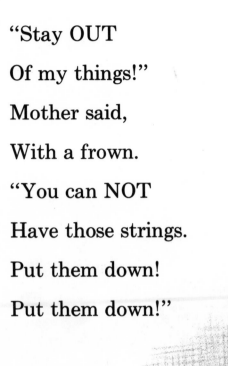

And my daddy has string.

Look what a lot!

Did he give ME some of it?

He did NOT.

"That is NOT a toy!
Put it down!"
Said Dad.

And — boy, oh, boy!
Was
  my
    dad
      MAD!

9

So I went out back,

To the big old cans.

There were socks and sacks,

And pots and pans.

I looked and looked.

And what did I see?

Strings and STRINGS,

And all for me!

But — here came a man,

And he shook out the can.

He shook all the things

From the can in a sack.

He took all the things

In a pack on his back.

"Hey! You with the sack!
You bring back my string!"

He did NOT bring it back.
He did not say a thing.

Away went the man.

Away went the truck.

And away I went!

And then — what luck!

BUMPETY-BUMP!

The truck dumped

With a thump.

And there I was

At the good old dump!

With bags of rags,

And old tin cans.

And mops and mats,

And pots and pans.

And jacks and tires,

And sacks and wires.

And cots and springs —

And lots

And LOTS

Of things

With STRINGS!

19

I put all the string

On my little string ball.

I made me the BIGGEST

String ball of all.

My ball was so big!

As big as my head!

And I looked

At my big ball of string,

And I said,

"NOW I will find

A thing of some kind —

Some GOOD kind of thing

To do with my string!"

I had a balloon like a pig

From the Zoo.

My balloon was so red and so big

And so new

That I said, "NOW I know

What will be a good thing!"

And I let my pig go

Up, up, UP, with my string!

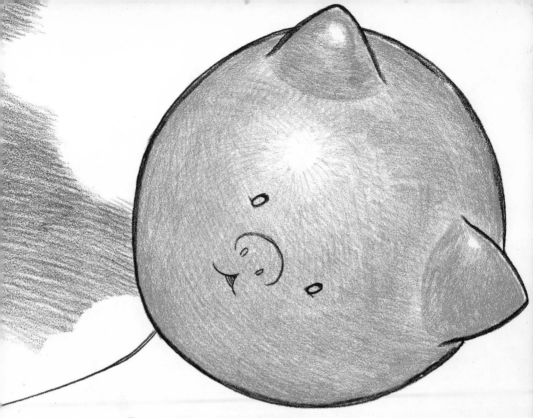

It went up so high

It was something to see!

As high as a house!

As high as a tree!

As high as the sky!

And I said, "Stop! Stop!

You are up TOO HIGH!"

And then, something went —

It went POP, like that!

My big red pig!

Then it was not fat,

Or red, or big.

It was all in bits,

And the bits fell on me.

And the string fell, too,

And got stuck in a tree.

So I went up the tree

To get down my string.

And I said, "Now I see

That was NOT a good thing!"

But I did not mind.

I KNEW I could find

Some good kind of thing

To do with my string.

So I got my string down

And I made a machine,

With a bike and a trike

And a jeep in between.

And I sat way up top,

On a box with a mop,

On the jeep in between,

And I ran the machine!

Then the bike hit a bump.

And the jeep gave a jump.

And the trike hit a tree.

And the box

And the mop

Came down,

KER-FLOP!

Came down

On top

Of ME!

So I got a big bump

On the top of my head.

And it made a big lump.

And I sat there and said,

"That was NOT a good thing

To do with my string,

With my string in a ball.

Not a good thing AT ALL!"

But I did not mind.

I KNEW I would find

Some good kind of thing

To do with my string.

Then I went up to bed.

"Tomorrow," I said,

"I will take my string out.

I will look all about.

I will FIND a good thing

To do with my string.

That is what I will do

Tomorrow," I said.

And I lay down to sleep,

With my string on my bed.

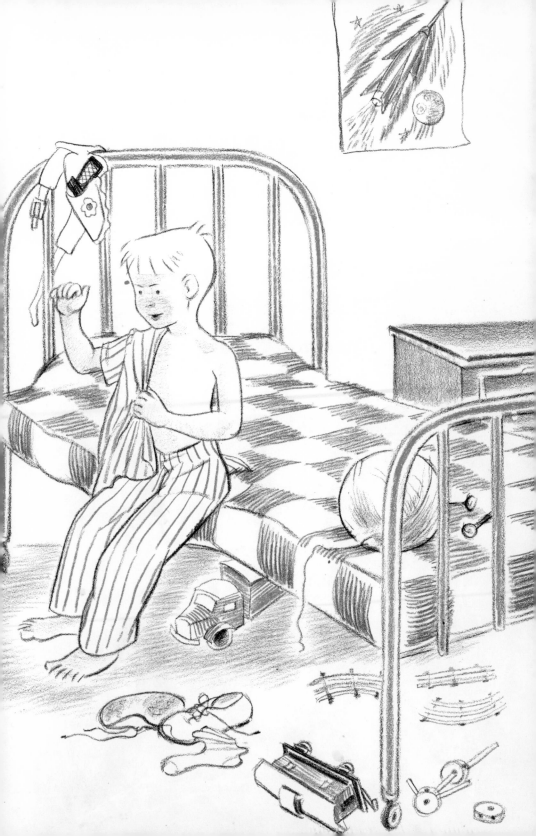

But THEN I woke up
With a cold in my head.

And my mother came in,

And she said,

"Stay in bed.

With a cold in your head,

Stay in bed!

Stay in bed!"

I shot all my darts
At the wall, and I said,
"Now how can I get them,
And stay in my bed?"

Then I looked at my string,

At my big ball of string.

And I said,

"NOW I know

What will be a good thing!

I can stay

In my bed

With my big ball of string!

I can play

In my bed!

I can do ANYTHING!"

With my string on my darts,

I can shoot them away!

I can get them all back!

I can do it all day!

I can shoot them about,

At the door,

At the wall.

I can shoot them all out

On the floor

In the hall!

I can shoot all my darts.

But — when they are shot,

I MAY want to look

At some books

I have got.

I can rig up a thing

With a box and a hook

And my big ball of string.

It will bring me a book.

And I can have fun

With my books

In my bed,

With my string,

And my gun,

And my cold in the head!

But the light should be right
When I look at my book.

I can pull up the blind
On this good sunny day.
I can turn on the light
If the sun goes away.
I can look at my book.
I can stay in my bed
With my gun, and my string,
And my cold in the head.

Then — I MAY want the cat.

She will come to the door.

She will jump at the mouse

On the string on the floor.

If I pull the door shut,

She can NOT run away.

I can play with the cat

In my bed all the day.

With my cat, and my gun,

And my books in my bed,

I can have lots of fun

With a cold in my head.

51

But — IF I get cold

With my cat in my bed,

I will want my old gown

That is woolly and red.

So when I get cold

I can let the string down.

I can stay in my bed

As I put on my gown.

With my cat,

And my gun,

And my books,

And my string,

I can have lots of fun.

I can do ANYTHING!

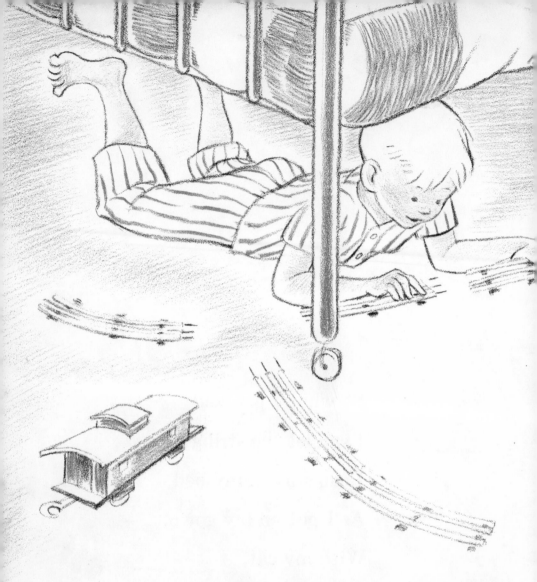

In my bed

With my string,

I can make my train go.

I can make it go fast.

I can make it go slow.

In my bed

With my books,

And my train on a string,

And my cat, and my gun,

I can do ANYTHING!

I will stay in my bed,

And I WILL not get out.

If I want anything

I will NOT run about.

I can rig up my bell

With my big ball of string.

My mother will come

When she hears the bell ring.

And THEN she will see

How I stay in my bed

With my strings,

And my things,

And my cold in the head!

Then Mother called up
To my room,
And she said,
"How is your cold?
DID YOU STAY IN YOUR BED?"

"Yes, Mother,"

I said.

And I JUMPED into bed.

I jumped into bed

With my string in a ball.

With my string,

With my string,

I can do ANYTHING.

Anything, anything,

ANYTHING AT ALL!

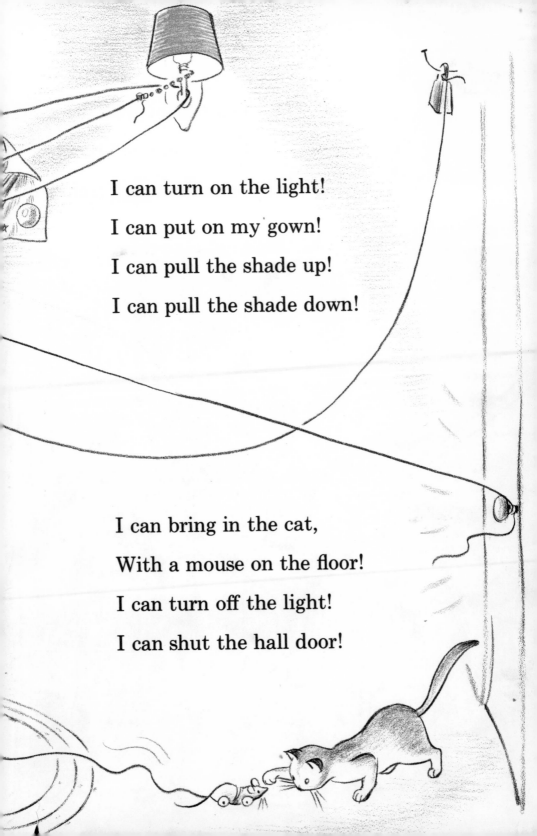

I can turn on the light!

I can put on my gown!

I can pull the shade up!

I can pull the shade down!

I can bring in the cat,

With a mouse on the floor!

I can turn off the light!

I can shut the hall door!

I can look at my book!

I can shoot with my gun!

I make my bell ring!

I can make my train run!

"Look, Mother!

Look, Mother!

LOOK, MOTHER!"

I said.

"Come and look,

Come and look,

How I stay in my bed,

With my strings,

And my things,

And my cold in the head!"

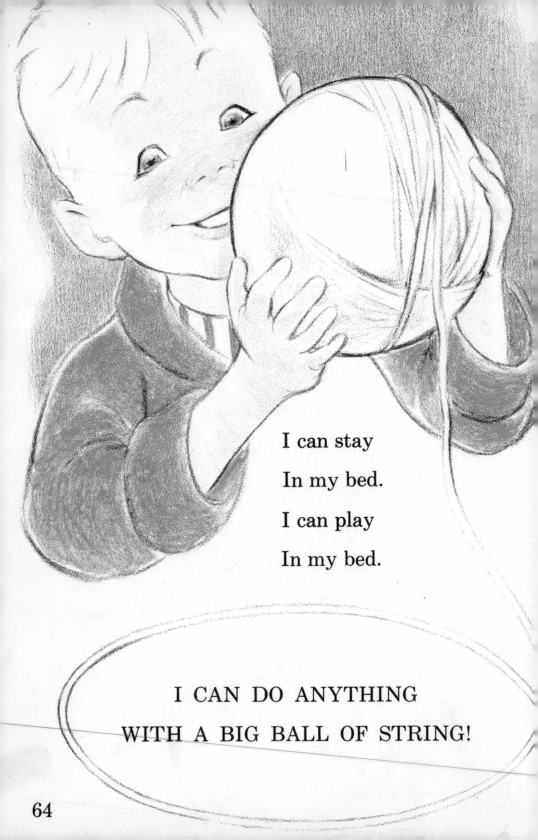

I can stay
In my bed.
I can play
In my bed.

I CAN DO ANYTHING
WITH A BIG BALL OF STRING!

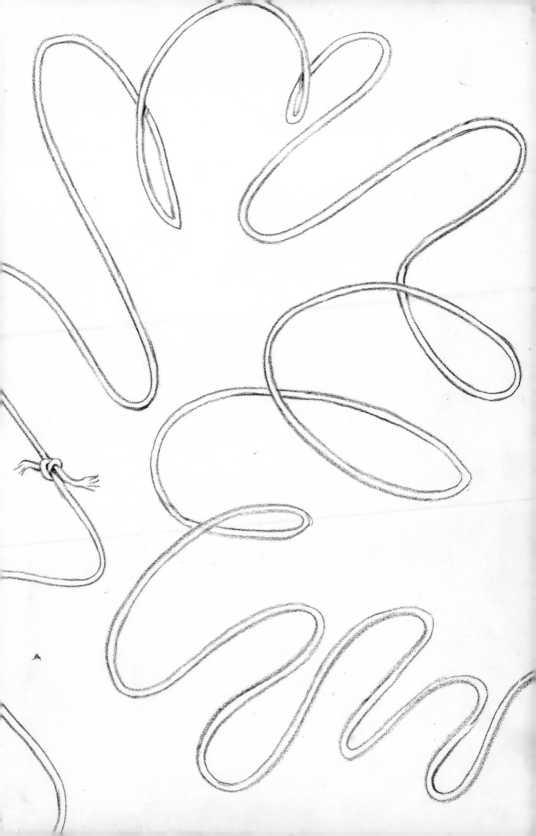